The School for
Laughter

Terry Denton

Houghton Mifflin Company

Boston 1990

Eddie was a happy little boy.

He was always laughing and
playing funny games.
He even smiled as he slept.

But one morning Eddie woke to find he had lost his laugh.

He tried very hard, but could not even manage a small smile.

Eddie searched high and low, but he couldn't find his laugh anywhere.

Eddie's laugh had disappeared.

His parents and little brother tried to amuse Eddie, but Eddie couldn't see what was so funny. After all, there's nothing to smile about when you've lost your laugh.

When after many days Eddie's laugh did not return, his parents became worried. Would their solemn son ever smile again?

Then Eddie's mother read about an unusual school — the School for Laughter, where children were encouraged to laugh and have a good time. This seemed the answer to the problem, and Eddie was soon enrolled.

On his first day Eddie's
new teacher, Miss Guffaw,
met him at the school
entrance.

They went inside and Miss Guffaw introduced Eddie
to his new classmates.

The School for Laughter was a happy place.

But Eddie was the most serious of students.

He enjoyed the games at recess, but never laughed or smiled.

Cooking classes were often messy.

And Eddie loved science class where
the children were allowed to conduct
interesting experiments.

But as the end of the school year drew near, Eddie still had not laughed.

His teachers became concerned. What
could they do to make Eddie laugh?

Some of Eddie's classmates decided to perform a few of their funniest tricks especially for Eddie. Perhaps this would help him laugh.

Stephen's shark impersonation was very
good.

Jane and Max dressed in a giraffe suit and danced on rollerskates.

Then the whole group performed funny acrobatics.

But still Eddie did not laugh.

A great gloom descended over the School for
Laughter. Eddie wished and wished he could find
his laugh. He couldn't bear to see his friends and
teachers looking so defeated.

He decided to find some of his old jokes to tell his friends. He rummaged through the case he'd brought to the school but had never opened.

Suddenly everyone heard a small chuckle from inside the case.

Eddie had found his laugh!

And now Eddie started to chuckle, shyly at first, but soon he was laughing heartily.

The end-of-year break-up party was the best — and most hilarious — ever. All the students received a prize.

And Miss Guffaw told Eddie's parents that their son had one of the happiest laughs she'd ever heard.

"The School for Laughter had nothing to teach him," Miss Guffaw said as she farewelled the family. "Eddie had just mislaid his laugh. I'm sure he'll not lose it again."

Eddie went home and back to a more ordinary school.

And he never lost his laugh again.

Library of Congress Cataloging-in-Publication Data

Denton, Terry.
    The school for laughter/Terry Denton. — 1st American ed.
        p.   cm.
    Summary: When Eddie loses his laugh, his parents send him to the
School of Laughter to get it back.
    ISBN 0-395-53353-8
    [1. Laughter—Fiction.] I. Title.
PZ7.D4374Sc   1990   89-26744
[E]—dc20   CIP
                                    AC

Printed in Hong Kong

10 9 8 7 6 5 4 3 2 1

*The Author would like to thank Rita Scharf of Oxford University Press for
her assistance in developing the book, and Michael Janover for the idea of a
school for laughter.*